The Castle

Nikki Moyes

Author: Moyes, Nikki

Title: **The Castle**/*Nikki Moyes.*

ISBN: 9780648514947 (paperback)

For girls everywhere, whatever your strengths may be.

The Castle

I breathed silently as I peered through the slits of the air vent into the Castle Conquest Room below. Cold air swirled around me and I shivered in my sleeveless tunic dress.

Below me stood the hulking form of Kyllar of Arna City, more commonly known as Class Three Warlord Kllrarn, as warlord names were traditionally reduced to a single vowel in an effort to sound more menacing.

I'd followed him after his meeting with Father that morning. My fists clenched, fingernails digging into my palms, at the memory of how easily Father had caved to Kllrarn's demands.

Powerless, that's what I was, even more so than Father, because I was female and not yet fully grown. People assumed I knew nothing, could achieve nothing worthwhile.

That's why I hid in a tight air duct system observing a man I usually went out of my way to avoid. I had Father's scientific mind when it came to problems. I would observe until a solution presented itself.

Kllrarn headed a squad of heavily armed warriors. The capacity of the dimly-lit room limited players to one hundred, although occasionally the door opened to admit an additional man, and I caught a glimpse of more loitering outside.

My eyes flicked over them, taking in the details of the thick leather trousers and shirts under tight-linked chain mail. Most wore wide belts slung with large leather pouches, as well as their usual swords, knives, and shields.

I wriggled forward in the narrow air duct until the monitor came into sight. The glow of the active screen reflected off the polished black walls and floor. My bare shoulder pressed against the cold metal tube and I flinched.

Kllrarn spoke loudly and slowly to the program which did the same thing in return whenever Kllrarn tried to skip a step.

'That request is not possible. Please state which level you would like to attempt.' The game's gender-neutral tone stated.

I smothered a grin and wondered if the game's creator, Warlord Waldn, based the program on someone he'd known personally.

"Castle Two, you incompetent piece of machinery," Kllrarn growled, swiping a beefy hand through his unruly, dark hair. "As soon as I'm married to that damned Suri girl, I'll make her fix this idiotic program so it does what I want," he muttered to his men.

I drew back from the vent as far as I could without losing sight of the room below. My body tensed in a flight, fight or freeze response, and sweat beaded on my forehead despite the cold air. My ears filled with the sound of my pounding heart.

"She's just a little kid. What would she know about fixing…" Rakon, one of Kllrarn's commanders, glanced at the monitoring screen beside them, "…stuff?"

"She's Sci. Suri's daughter. She has his memories in her head or something," Kllrarn snapped.

"So she's like the same as Suri?" Another warrior asked. "Wouldn't that be like marrying Suri, himself? Wouldn't make for a fun wedding night, now would it?"

His laughter was cut short as Kllrarn buried his knife into the man's gut. He made a brief gurgling sound and collapsed on the shiny black floor.

Kllrarn bent down to wipe his knife clean on the man's trousers, before he returned it to its sheath and turned his attention back to the screen. I covered my mouth and swallowed the bile rising in my throat.

"Get him out of here and send in the next man," Rakon instructed the wary warriors standing nearby.

Two stepped forward and grabbed the dying man under the armpits. They dragged him outside the room and returned moments later with a replacement warrior.

"If I control her, I control Suri Technology, see?" Kllrarn continued as though he hadn't been interrupted. "Then I won't have to pay for all these weapons, get it? I'm sick of that scrawny, little man telling me he can't make me projectile weapons because the Ethics Committee said it was bad." Kllrarn thumped his fist against the wall.

Do you wish to exit?' The program asked helpfully.

"NO!" Kllrarn bellowed. "I want to capture the castle!"

'All participants must take their place.'

"They will when I'm good and ready," he growled, although he waved at his men to move into position.

"Damn funny watching Suri shaking in his fancy white coat when you threatened to rip his brains out through his nose." Rakon made a swirling motion as though using a tool to carry out the threat. The men around him laughed and even Kllrarn's shoulders relaxed marginally.

Each of Kllrarn's warriors stepped into an individual square marked on the floor. A shimmering barrier surrounded them as one by one their minds entered the virtual world. The noise from the room died away, to be replaced by the screen's speakers recording the game.

Kllrarn was last to step into his square at the front of the room. Moments later his image appeared at the head of his hundred-strong army within sight of Castle Two. Their physical bodies remained motionless on the squares marked out on the floor.

For a brief moment, I fantasied about sneaking down into the room and ending Kllrarn's life with a swift knife attack like he had just carried out. I could probably get in and out of the room without anyone knowing until they found his body.

But I was not a killer. I could never take a life, even one like Kllrarn.

From my vantage point, I watched the wall-sized display screen as virtual Kllrarn marched on the castle he had attempted to capture twice before. Time moved faster in the program and I attempted to estimate how long Kllrarn would need to capture the castle.

An explosion blossomed across the screen in flashes of red and orange that cast shadows across the motionless warriors in the room. My heart beat faster. The outer Castle Two wall cracked. If Kllrarn destroyed the castle, it would eliminate the level from the game and he would be that bit more unstoppable in his pursuit of power.

Kllrarn directed several more explosives against Castle Two's walls before it occurred to me that the men below me carried the actual live weapons in the pouches on their belts.

I wriggled quickly back through the narrow tube system to the grate I came in through. The corridor of the Warlord Training Facility below was silent and I lifted the grate, slipped through stepping on the strategically placed cleaning cart, and tugged the cover back into place. I jumped down to the floor. My next growth spurt would most likely prevent me crawling through the ducts again.

I shoved the cleaning cart away from the vent and walked quickly down the corridor. As I rounded the corner, I almost collided with a cloaked figure walking beside Training Master Zander. The hooded man was almost as tall as the aging warlord trainer, although he possessed the slender build of someone who didn't fight for a living.

"Risha, I wasn't expecting to see you here today." Zander broke the silence of me staring at the Dragon Temple Keeper.

"Why are you here, Takarna?" I asked the Keeper, ignoring Zander.

"Castle One is about to fall for the first time in history. The new warlord will be known as The Destroyer and I see the person being influential in the direction our world will take. I felt Training Master Zander should be aware of the development," Takarna Orlan replied in his melodic tone.

Shivers slid over my body as my mind flashed back to Kllrarn in the Conquest Room. The men waiting outside the room must be replacements so he could take Castle One as soon as he had finished with Castle Two. The destruction I witnessed of Castle Two certainly fit the description.

Time slipped away from me. I needed help if I was to avoid the deal my father made with Kllrarn, preferably without Father having his brain removed through his nostrils. Kllrarn would be virtually unstoppable as a Class One Warlord. My chest constricted in a moment of panic, and I shuffled my feet, eager to get out of there.

"You expect us to believe some vision you've had?" I asked.

"Your brother believes, although he didn't at first, too occupied with trying to see the science in everything instead of surrendering to faith."

"You two know each other?" Zander glanced between the pair of us.

"Her twin, Ritash, is my apprentice," Takarna Orlan said.

Zander gave me a look of surprise.

"Ah, I see you weren't aware she has a brother."

"Risha doesn't say much about family, just turned up when she was barely five-years-old begging to be taught self-defence. I look out for her when I can. Never had the opportunity to have children myself," Zander replied.

The Keeper reached out and touched his fingertips to my bare cheek. A tingle started in the back of my mind like an itch about to form. I blinked up at him and he dropped his hand.

"Interesting, your mind appears to be deviating from that of your brother. I suspect I'll be seeing more of you in the future." Takarna Orlan nodded his head once as though agreeing with himself and then vanished.

"How does he do that?" Zander muttered as he waved a hand through the empty space the Keeper had occupied moments ago.

"No idea." I wondered if my twin Tash knew, and for a moment jealousy attempted to worm itself into my mind for the knowledge I didn't possess.

"I figured you'd make yourself scarce with Kllrarn here today," Zander said.

"I'm not planning on running into him. Shouldn't you be monitoring his attempt to make history?" My voice remained steady, but my thumb and finger tapped together in a tiny repetitive motion.

"Castle Two hasn't been captured in thirty years and Castle One is infallible," Zander said. "It can't be conquered with a hundred men and Kllrarn has the IQ of a cumquat. I'll read the highlights when he withdraws."

"You don't believe in the Keeper's vision?" I took a few steps forward as the sense of time slipping away settled over me again.

"No." Zander took another look at me. "What on Lordinia are you wearing?"

I wiped my hands over my course brown tunic dress in an attempt to remove the grime from my recent excursion through the air conditioning ducts.

"There's a fancy dress party in Central Zone. I'm going as a peasant girl." I clasped my hands behind my back. My eyes darted down the hall, but we were still alone.

"I honestly can't imagine you at a party with other twelve-year-olds," Zander said.

"I never said the party was for people my age."

"My mistake, maybe one day you will trust me sufficiently to share whose genetic memory you were born with."

"I don't know what you're talking about." I opened my eyes wide in my best innocent look. "You might want to check on Kllrarn. His men have brought some pretty powerful explosives into the Castle Conquest Room. You may need to evacuate the entire building."

An annoyed look crossed Zander's features and he hurried off in Kllrarn's direction. As soon as he was out of sight, I darted into a different hallway.

I almost ran into a warrior near the dining hall, but I ducked down a secondary hallway before he saw me, ending up in a wing of the original building with its mostly unused rooms.

I checked the signs above the doors and tried the handle of one unused room. I slipped inside, turned the lock and rested my head against the door of the tiny room, taking deep breaths and focusing on the cool, smooth surface until my heartbeat was no longer the loudest sound in the room.

My nose itched with the musty, disused air. A motion activated monitoring system hummed quietly against the wall.

'Welcome, Player One. Do you wish to conquer Castle Ten?' It greeted me as I stepped away from the door.

I scanned the tiny room. A small screen was mounted on the far wall, its red-lit camera following my movements. Several chairs were stacked in a corner beside a table as though the room had been used for storing excess study room furniture.

"Is it safe…from warlords?" I asked.

'Castle Ten is the base level. It is the most frequent castle conquered by warlords.'

"That doesn't sound safe." I dragged the table towards the door.

'Do you require protection?' The program's tone became gentler and less official. I shoved the table into place and turned to face the screen.

"You know someone who can protect me from Warlord Kllrarn?"

'Class One Warlord Waldn resides at Castle One. Class Three Kllrarn is no match for him.'

"Won't someone notice if I enter the virtual world?"

'A conquest is currently in progress. Your entry will go unnoticed.'

"How do I get to Castle One?" I allowed the hitch in my voice to be heard. It was the sound of a young girl who needed protection.

'Standby...'

I wiped my sweaty palms on my rough tunic dress.

*Full name...*The words appeared across the screen.

"Tarish, daughter of Suri."

I tapped my finger and thumb together as the out-of-date system scanned the room. The light travelled over me twice before a rendered image of myself appeared on the screen.

My image rotated so I could see my brown dress, sandals, and the brightly coloured butterfly clip holding my hair off my face.

'Step forward when ready.'

I crossed the worn carpeted floor and the world flickered around me. A faint whirring sounded in my ears before the room faded away.

I appeared at the edge of a dense forest, the trees a vivid combination of browns and green with hints of rainbows when I caught sight of a flower. My home city of Lordinia outgrew its green spaces a long time ago. Father still recalled the time before when plants, insects and little creatures existed, which was where his interest in genetics first developed.

To my left, thick black smoke billowed from Castle Two into the pale blue, cloudless sky. The sounds of distant screams drifted towards me on the breeze.

Ahead in the distance, Castle One stood in the open. Its appearance was similar to a child's book Zander once gave me before he caught me reading the *Warlord Rules of War* from his office.

I slipped back into the trees. Staying among the foliage would take longer but limit the chance of Kllrarn's men noticing me.

Near the outer edge of the forest, my foot caught a tree root, sending me sprawling. I rolled several times, a sharp stick ripping the hem of my dress and cutting my leg, until I came to a sudden wet splash in a small stream. I shook the cold water from my ears in disgust and ran a hand down my face.

For a moment I trailed my fingers through the stream, marvelling at the realistic sensation of temperature and texture, as though I was actually sitting in cold water that stung as it flowed over my injured leg.

I hauled myself up the muddy bank. A narrow trail of blood trickled down my thigh from the gash. The strap on one sandal hung by a thread and strands of wet hair fell across my dirty face where they escaped from my mud-covered butterfly hairclip.

A series of distant horn blasts from the army indicated they were on the move. I listened carefully to the codes. Kllrarn was gathering his remaining men and the reinforcements for an assault on Castle One.

I dropped to my knees and covered my head with my hands as Father's memories invaded my mind — the fear he felt towards Kllrarn made my entire body tremble.

"I am not you, Father," I hissed between clenched teeth. "I am Risha. I will not be afraid," I repeated as I blocked out the genetic memory until it was only me in my mind.

I forced myself to my feet and wrapped a stray lock of hair around my finger. Father kept his hair short and neat. Mine grew long for when I needed to remember I was my own person.

The dark plume of smoke billowed across the fertile land. At the edge of the forest, there was nothing between me and Castle One but my fear and rough open plain. Behind me unseen, an army marched towards my location.

I hiked my skirt up and ran, watching the ground to avoid twisting an ankle in the knee-high grass. The strap on my left sandal snapped and I tripped, grazing my shoulder as I tucked into a protective ball and tumbled through the rough grass. I glanced behind me as I struggled to my feet, kicking the broken shoe away. I kept running, although now it was more of a hurried limp.

When I reached the heavy outer timber entrance scored with the mark of Warlord Class One, I beat my fists against the small door set into the right-hand gate. The guards were shadows above me on the stone wall that stretched away in either direction. For a brief moment, the wall shimmered and I received a tiny electric shock. I jerked my hand away.

"Help! Help me! The soldiers are coming! Please, help..." I screamed.

I glanced back towards the forest. In the distance a cloud of dust heralded Warlord Kllrarn's advance. I'd misjudged the time it would take him to cover the distance between castles.

I rested my forehead against the barrier, my heart hammering in my chest. The wind blew, chilling the sweat on my body. The ground around the castle was cleared, making it impossible to retreat from the approaching army undetected. I kicked the door as tears slipped down my face, I was out of time. I'd never be free of Kllrarn.

The door gave way and I fell to my knees inside the entrance. Several hands reached out to haul me to my feet as the door banged shut behind us.

"She's just a child," a soldier said. I looked up through wet lashes at the hulking warrior and his three heavily armed companions.

"What are you doing here?" his commanding officer demanded, aiming his projectile weapon casually at the ground.

"Everything on fire, people screaming, soldiers everywhere." I waved a hand in the direction of the plume of smoke. "I lost my shoe," I added, pointing at my filthy foot.

"Get her inside. Kllrarn's army will be here shortly," the commanding officer ordered his men.

"Yes, sir."

Several women stationed within the inner wall took me from the men. A tall woman with short cropped hair and the form-fitting black uniform of a warrior ran her hands down my sides. My tunic dress had no pockets and I carried nothing but my butterfly clip, dull with the mud in my hair.

"She's not a player." She nodded her head and another woman wrapped a blanket around my shoulders muttering soothing words. She led me inside the fortified castle.

"What's your name, child?" she asked gently.

"Tarish, but everyone calls me Risha." I glanced around me, taking in every detail of the inside of the castle.

Various children stared at me before someone ushered them away. The castle occupants that weren't built like warriors tended to animals, carried supplies for the people up on the wall, or went about the general running of the community within the castle boundaries.

"Why are there so many women and children here?" I asked.

"Lord Waldn offers us sanctuary," the woman replied.

"From men like Kllrarn?"

"Yes, my dear, protection from warlords, abusive husbands, forced marriages and such."

"But if they stay here, what happens to their bodies in the real world?"

"They die, I suppose. It's not like there's anyone in them anymore to keep them functioning. A physical body isn't needed here."

She led me past sleeping quarters and ushered me into an open bathing room. A young girl hurried away to fetch a clean outfit while I stripped behind a screen and lowered myself into the warm water of a bathtub. The woman picked up a bag beside a chair in the corner of the room and started repairing a shirt.

"Why was that woman dressed like the warriors?" I quickly washed the mud from my limbs and hair, turning the water a murky brown.

"Lydia is one of our best fighters."

I paused to stare at her around the edge of the privacy screen. "Father believes females can never achieve the greatness of a male."

I waited for her answer with my pulse pounding in my wrists. Father had his company; my twin was destined to become the Keeper of the Dragon Temple. Was I destined to merely be a female related to them? Father's disappointment over my gender twisted my insides and confused the logical part of my brain.

"What a cart load of horse manure!" the woman exclaimed. "We all have our strengths and weaknesses. They have more to do with our upbringing and interests, than genitalia."

If Father was wrong, were there other things he could be wrong about? If I could correct his flaws, I could be a better version of us instead of merely a continuation of his knowledge. I could take control of his genetic experiment and make it my own.

I refastened my cleaned butterfly into my freshly washed hair before pulling on the offered leggings and slipped the green shift dress over my head. A boom sounded as Kllrarn's army began their assault on Castle One. My body tensed.

"Are we safe here?" My voice wobbled. The woman smiled.

"This city is impenetrable. Come, I'll take you to see Lord Waldn."

"The creator of this world?"

"Yes, he likes to meet all new arrivals to our castle."

She took my hand, tugging me along behind her as we climbed the spiral stair to the central tower. I caught glimpses of Kllrarn's army and Castle One's defenders as we passed narrow windows. The woman tapped on the door at the top, bowing as she pulled me in behind her.

"M'Lord Waldn, this is Risha." The woman dropped my hand and nudged me forward.

I stared at the man before me. He had chosen to remain in his prime, perhaps around thirty years of age. He stood straight and tall, with a surprising kindness on his face for the most powerful warlord to have ever lived.

"Don't stare, girl." The woman gently slapped my arm.

"I've never met anyone who died and still exists," I said. Warlord Waldn laughed.

"Only my body died. When I downloaded my consciousness into my program, I continued to live. You can leave us be, Anna-Lee."

"As you wish, M'Lord."

The woman backed out, closing the door behind her. I was left alone with the man who created the virtual world. The science was fascinating, and I bit my tongue to prevent myself asking technical questions a twelve-year-old would fail to understand.

"Who's the woman?" I pointed to the painting of a smiling woman dressed in black pants and shirt similar to what Lydia wore. The belt around her waist contained a variety of knives, and a faint scar marked the brown skin of her left arm.

"My wife, Nadia," Waldn said with a hint of sadness in his voice. "She died before I finished this world and so she is lost to me forever. She was the best warrior I have ever known."

"Father says that girls can never be as strong as males."

My brother and I were born knowing everything Father knew and one of those facts was that females were inherently weaker, less intelligent. I'd existed for twelve years with this conflict in my head like an unbalanced equation.

"Nadia was the strongest and smartest person I have ever known. Never let a man make you believe that you can't achieve your goals."

"I could never take on someone like Kllrarn." I tapped my fingers together.

Waldn's words confirm Anna-Lee's belief, but the mind could be stubborn when it came to rejecting previous beliefs.

Waldn looked me up and down for a moment then waved me over to the window. I moved to his side and followed the direction his finger pointed.

"What is Kllrarn's strength?" Waldn asked.

I looked out over the castle wall to the army below. A castle archer hit one of Kllrarn's men and the wounded man disappeared from the game. The archer took his time reloading. The muscles in Kllrarn's bulky body rippled as he bellowed at his men.

"He is strong," I replied.

"What is his weakness?"

I looked again, but all I could think about was Father cowering before the warlord. I shrugged.

"The man is slow and lacks flexibility. He also lacks intelligence. A warrior who is fast, flexible, and smart could strike at him first. Their speed would allow them to avoid many of his hits. Always exploit the weakness of your enemy in a battle," Waldn said.

I considered his words for a moment. "Can the castle be taken?"

"The castle learns from each attack and modifies itself accordingly. It cannot be invaded."

"They have explosives. Kllrarn has already destroyed Castle Two."

Waldn's face tightened briefly. "I have been made aware of his actions, and Castle One has modified its protective shields in response. His weapons will not be effective this time."

I frowned slightly. I was not familiar with the capabilities of the game's program, but I was familiar with the specifications of the weapons Kllrarn's men carried.

"Why doesn't he focus on capturing the flag instead of trying to bring down the walls?" I glanced at Waldn's flag flying proudly from a turret visible from our window; a bird with outstretched wings over the top of the elaborate swirling Warlord Circle. My mind pondered designs for a flying drone to reach the flag undetected.

"It probably never occurred to him, not that it would do him any good."

"Why?"

"That one's a decoy." Waldn grinned, crinkles forming at the corners of his eyes.

"Oh." I returned to looking out of the window at the assault below. After some time, I spoke again. "Why did you put a sparrow on your flag?"

"It's an eagle." Waldn leaned forward to peer at his flag, fingers drumming agitatedly on the window sill.

"Why does it have a worm in its claws?" I kept my tone innocent.

"That's a snake," Waldn growled.

"Doesn't look like it from here." I leaned against the window as if getting closer would reveal an eagle with a snake instead of a sparrow and worm. My fingers left sweat marks where they rested on the sill.

I flinched when the next explosion spread across the castle wall. A slight vibration ran through the building but no damage appeared. I stepped away from the window, not wanting to see Kllrarn's army any more.

"The real flag comes out when someone new arrives so they can swear fealty to Castle One and the protection of its people..." His voice trailed off as I wandered the room tracing my fingers over furniture and objects. "Why are you here?"

I hesitated at the question and glanced quickly at the window before resuming my study of the room.

"I didn't mean to come here. I was hiding from Kllrarn."

"I doubt a man like that would notice a small girl like you," Waldn tried to reassure me. I shook my head.

"Father signed an agreement with Kllrarn..." I swallowed and focused on taking deep breaths. "He promised me to Kllrarn as soon as I reach sixteen standard rotations."

A frown of confusion spread across Waldn's face. "Why?"

"Kllrarn wants to control Father's company. Suri Technology is the largest technology producer in the galaxy," I replied.

"Ah, you'd be safe from Kllrarn if you wish to remain in my castle."

Waldn moved over to a bare section of wall behind us. He pulled a key from a chain around his neck, made several movements and a secret compartment slid open. He slipped the key into the lock and pulled out a neatly folded flag. My heart rate spiked.

He walked over to me with Castle One's flag in his hands. My fingers itched to touch it, but I snatched my hand back.

"Go on. Open it up." Waldn offered me the flag.

I stared at him wide-eyed before reaching out to take it from him. I carefully opened out the soft white fabric, resting it on a nearby table to keep it from touching the ground. An eagle with a snake in its beak flew across the circular design representing Waldn and the rank of Class One Warlord.

"It's beautiful," I whispered. "Aren't you worried someone might try to sneak in and take it?"

Waldn laughed. "No. It takes a certain type of person to become a warlord. They're easy to spot. My guards would never let them in."

"How do you pick them?"

"Well, the majority are male. They can't compete to capture a castle unless they hold a university degree, so it's rare to see anyone younger than twenty-two. They carry weapons and most walk with an exaggerated arrogance." He winked at me.

"You don't think Kllrarn can capture your castle?"

Waldn laughed again. "He uses aggression to get what he wants. By the time a contender has conquered the other nine levels, Castle One has already adapted itself to protect from their fighting style. The harder he fights, the stronger my castle becomes."

"But they don't have to conquer the castles in order, do they?" I hugged the soft fabric of the flag to my body.

"No, but if they fail a level, there is a time penalty before they can make the next attempt. Most warlords prefer to take each level in order rather than risking failure on a higher level." Waldn turned his back to me, glancing out the window once more.

I ran a hand through my hair, fingers catching on the butterfly clip. In one swift move, I pulled it from my bun and squeezed the butterfly's wings together. A blade flicked out. I kicked my right foot out catching Waldn in the back of the leg. He fell to his knees on the floor as my blade pressed to his throat.

"I capture your castle," I whispered in his ear, his flag clutched to my chest.

The world around us flickered like it had when I stood at the gate and the castle updated its defences.

"Why? I offered you protection."

"If I stay here, who's going to stop Kllrarn hurting people in the real world? I won't let him take Suri Technology from me."

"How old are you?" Waldn remained still against my knife.

"Twelve."

"How did you get around the qualification requirements?"

I grinned. "I was born with Father's memories. He has many degrees so the process is familiar to me. I have a Master's in Weapons Technology, and History of Weaponry."

I watched Class One Warlord Waldn's face in the window's reflection as it changed from confusion to something else entirely. He laughed and pushed my blade away from his neck. Then he stood and bowed to me.

"Congratulations Class One Warlord," he spluttered between fits of laughter. "What is your full name?"

"Tarish daughter of Suri."

"Then let it be known that Warlord Tarsh now controls Castle One. May you bring about Kllrarn's destruction."

About the Author

Nikki Moyes was born in Victoria and moved around Australia amassing an eclectic range of occupations including tallship watch leader, apiarist, rose farm hand, and sandwich artist. In her spare time she learns tissu, static trapeze, and aerial hoop (she couldn't decide on one) in case she needs to run off and join the circus.

You can find her here:

www.facebook.com/moyes.nikki/
www.instagram.com/nikkimoyesauthor/
www.goodreads.com/author/show/15606198.Nikki_Moyes

If you enjoyed Risha's story, please leave a review. Her story will continue in THE DESTROYER, but first, THE KEEPER – Book 1 of the Suri Series is out now.

Other books by Nikki Moyes

The Keeper – Book 1 of the Suri Series

17-year-old Cassie is pressured into a bachelorette-style program, but one of the contestants is keeping secrets about the mysterious disappearance of the Keeper of the Dragon Temple, and Governor Suri - ruler of the universe who was born with a thousand years of ancestral memories.

<u>Young Adult Fiction:</u>

If I Wake

The Keeper (Book 1 - Suri Series)

The Castle (Suri Series - short story)

The Halfling (Suri Series - short story)

<u>Fiction:</u>

The Dark Lord's Risk Assessor (short
story)

<u>Non-Fiction:</u>

Kokoda Trek: 75th Anniversary

<u>Picture Book:</u>

Let's Imagine What We Will Do

www.ingramcontent.com/pod-product-compliance
Lightning Source LLC
Chambersburg PA
CBHW070403120726
47909CB00008B/2971